Delight thyself also in the LORD: and he shall
give thee the desires of thine heart.

Psalm 37: 4

Dedications:

To our Heavenly Father who gave me a gift, a vision, and made it possible to develop both over the years, I give You the praise. You have made another dream come true and I humbly thank You.

For Jasmine and Jessica, two of the best daughters a father could ever hope for. Thank you for your creative input and inspiration.

For Kendell Lawrence Johnson, a little knight in the making.

In memory of Emilia Morgan Claytor.

ISBN: 1-4196-8285-7
Library of Congress Control Number: 2007909026
Publisher: BookSurge Publishing
North Charleston, South Carolina

Visit www.sirnickoftyme.com to order additional copies.

Sir Nick of Tyme

Written & Illustrated by Kevin Dove
Edited by Veronica Dove

 ong ago in a tiny hamlet called Tyme, children learned that great men must be strong and brave and that only the strongest and bravest of these were knighted. This captured the

imagination of every young lad. Hours were spent
imitating the brave acts of knights that were heard
about in bedtime stories. Such was the case for Nick,
the son of the town's most famous bakery chef.

Nick was a good boy. He was always polite and well mannered, addressing his elders with a "yes sir" or "ma'am." He didn't throw tantrums and he wasn't

known to make mischief. He studied hard and did his chores before playing. He helped his father gather spices for baking. Sometimes, Nick would get curious and secretly mix a few spices together just to see how it would taste.

play at being a knight, but often the other children would tease him. "A baker's son can never be a knight," the children laughed. "Who ever heard of a knight who baked cakes and pies?"

This hurt his feelings, but Nick never backed down. He boasted about the many ways he could save the town without ever raising a sword. He once said he would grow to be the richest fellow in Tyme by

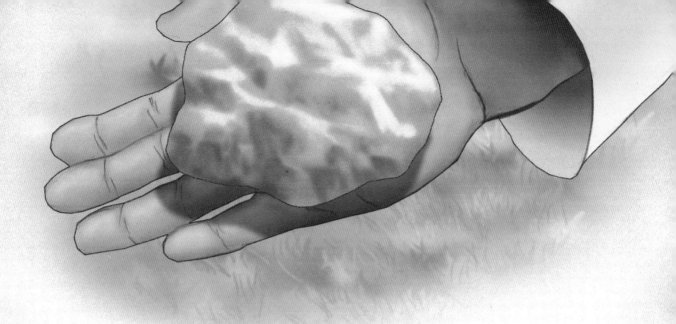

inventing a way to turn stone to gold. He promised to rid the town of beggars by giving each enough to buy food for a lifetime. Though these were fantasies, he loved speaking every word. It made him feel very important. After all, a baker's son could never be a knight. At least, that's what he was told.

Years later, when Nick grew up, he took over his father's bakery. He remembered everything his dad taught him and the flavors he discovered from mixing spices together when he was a boy. He treasured his dad's favorite saying, "Bake as if for a king and allow the poor a little taste of royalty." And so he did. He baked each item as if it was the best he ever made and at the end of the day, he baked a few extra treats for the poor.

Nick was not afraid to try something new. He would bake things no one had ever seen or tasted. His kindness and hard work were unmatched. Some even thought he was a better baker than his father.

At night, before going to bed, he gave thanks to God in his prayers and fell fast asleep. Sometimes he would find himself dreaming of being a knight just as he did when he was a boy. In the morning, he would awake feeling silly from the dream. "I will never be more than a baker," Nick would tell himself. Still he could not deny the desire in his heart to become a knight.

Meanwhile, on the other side of town, the king was preparing for his 25th anniversary as ruler of Tyme. He demanded to have the biggest royal anniversary feast ever. At first everything was running smoothly until the king's overzealous chef experimenting with a new "baking" powder blew out half of the royal kitchen with an exploding cake. This was very bad news for the chef for it was certain death for anyone who failed the king.

The king was a mountain of a man with an appetite greater than his size. It seemed that the smallest thing about him was his heart. He ruled with fear because he believed that was the only way to earn the respect and loyalty of the people. He was short on patience and had a terrible temper. And now that half of his kitchen was in ruins, he was meaner than ever and demanded the chef to be taken to the dungeon.

Those who disappoint his majesty were doomed to meet the hideous beast of the dungeon that had a fondness for the flavor of men. Legend had it that 13 knights were devoured before the creature was finally captured and that was just a snack.

After the chef was taken away, a royal message was sent into town and the crier read aloud the announcement. "His majesty seeks a new baker for the royal anniversary feast. He requires 100 loaves of bread, 75 cakes, and 50 pies to be ready in three days." It was an opportunity of a lifetime for the baker who could fulfill the king's request, but almost immediately the excitement turned to fear.

"Who could possibly fulfill that order in just three days?" cried one baker. "Surely, the king would feed us to the beast if we were one crumb short! Besides, no one beyond the castle walls has ever baked for royalty." Out of all the bakers in town, Nick was the only person brave enough to accept the challenge.

Nick never worked harder. He baked night and day for three days straight without so much as a nap. His eyes got so heavy that they were almost shut. His body was so tired that he could barely hold a spoon. But each time he felt he couldn't mix another bowl, Nick remembered his dad's favorite saying, "Bake as if for a king and allow the poor a little taste of royalty." This always gave him an extra boost of energy to keep going.

On the third day, without a second to spare, Nick pulled the last pie from the oven, just before the royal coach arrived. And like always, there were extra treats for the poor. The king was amazed by Nick's endurance and courage. He knew that no other baker was brave enough to accept his challenge for fear of the beast. But it was Nick's humility and kindness that touched him most. As the king arrived he watched as Nick handed the extra baked goods to the poor. He saw the respect and the love they gave willingly to Nick because of his kind deeds. This warmed the king's cold heart.

"Your goods may quiet my stomach," said the king, "but your generosity has filled my soul." So, like Nick he began to share. He gave each beggar he saw three pieces of gold and received something much more valuable in return; warm smiles of gratitude and a newfound feeling of respect from the people. He discovered that it was far more rewarding to treat people with kindness than to rule with a mean heart.

The king was so impressed with Nick's strength and bravery that he knighted him on that very day. Finally, Nick's dream had come true without ever lifting a sword. Because of Nick's example, the poor were given enough gold to buy food for a whole year without ever having to turn any stone to gold. From that day forth, Nick the baker's son became known as Sir Nick of Tyme and of course lived happily ever after.

The End.

Acknowledgements

I would like to thank the many who helped make this a reality through prayer, feedback, time, talent and encouragement.

Dr. C. Matthew Hudson, Jr. – My powerfully, praying Pastor

Deacon Bettie Sheppard – Assistant Editor

Michael Carter – Proofreader

Lawrence & Linda Dove, Melissa Jones, Harvey Webb, Belinda Davis, Monda Webb and the Matthews Memorial Baptist Church family.

Photography by Lifetouch

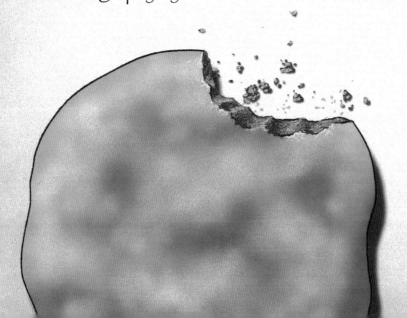

Veronica and Kevin Dove

About the Author:

As CEO/Creative Director and co-owner of DigiGraph Media in Silver Spring, Maryland, Kevin Dove performs the duties of lead 2D/3D animator, compositor and editor, bringing more than 20 years experience to his craft.

Mr. Dove is a graduate of the Corcoran College of Art and Design in Washington, DC. It was there that the first draft of Sir Nick of Tyme was created in the form of a coloring book.

Kevin is a devoted husband and father of two daughters and has served as a deacon at Matthews Memorial Baptist Church in Washington, DC. He and his family reside in Southern Maryland.

1503135